THE ILLUSTRATED COLLECTION

SIR ARTHUR CONAN DOYLE

SHERLOCK HOLMES

Dados Internacionais de Catalogação na Publicação (CIP) de acordo com ISBD

D754s Doyle, Arthur Conan
A study in scarlet / Arthur Conan Doyle; ilustrado por Arianna Bellucci. - Jandira, SP : Ciranda Cultural, 2023.
216 p. ; il; 13,20cm x 20,00cm. (The Illustrated Collection).

ISBN: 978-85-380-9208-7

1. Literatura inglesa. 2. Aventura. 3. Detetive. 4. Mistério. 5. Suspense. I. Bellucci, Arianna. II. Título. III. Série.

CDD 823.91
2022-0447 CDU 821.111-3

Elaborado por Lucio Feitosa - CRB-8/8803

Índice para catálogo sistemático:
1. Literatura inglesa 823.91
2. Literatura inglesa 821.111-3

Based on the original story from Sir Arthur Conan Doyle, adapted by Stephanie Baudet
Cover designed by Arianna Bellucci and Rhiannon Izard
Illustrations by Arianna Bellucci

1st edition in 2023
www.cirandacultural.com.br

THE ILLUSTRATED COLLECTION

A STUDY IN SCARLET

SCAN THE CODE TO HEAR THE STORY!

Ciranda Cultural

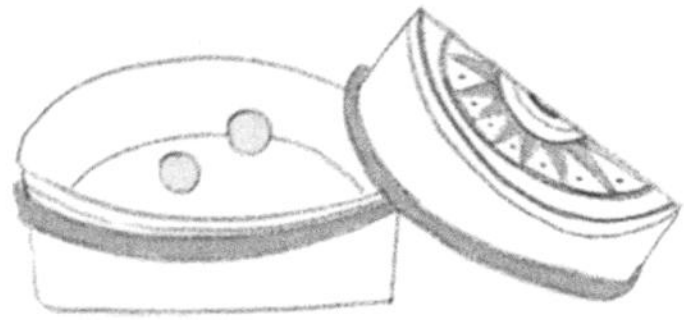

Chapter One

I met Sherlock Holmes by chance. It seems strange to me that such random occurrences may have such an impact on the direction of one's life, but that is precisely what happened that day in London.

I had returned to the city in 1879 after a bullet wound in my shoulder had ended my career as an army surgeon. My pension barely covered the expense of keeping a room at a hotel, and my health was too fragile for me to find work as a doctor.

I was having a drink at the Criterion Bar and considering how to find cheaper lodgings when someone tapped me on the shoulder. I turned to see young Stamford, who had assisted me when I was a doctor at St Bartholomew's Hospital.

It was good to see a familiar face, so I invited him to lunch.

We hailed a hansom cab and as we rattled through the busy London streets, I told him briefly about my adventures until we reached a restaurant. As we

Hansom cab

A quick and relatively cheap mode of public transport, just right for two people. It can take corners fast without tipping over, despite having only two wheels. The driver sits outside at the back of the carriage, so that passengers are able to have a private conversation.

Another choice is the Clarence cab. These have four wheels and are called 'growlers' because of the noise they make over cobbles. They are useful for groups of more than two, or if taking luggage.

talked, I realised just how lonely I had been.

'You poor devil,' Stamford said as we seated ourselves at a table and reached for the menu. 'Your injuries must still bother you. What are you up to now?'

'Looking for lodgings,' I answered. 'And wondering whether it is possible to get comfortable rooms at a reasonable price.'

'How strange,' said Stamford. 'You are the second man to tell me that today.'

'And who was the first?' I asked.

'A fellow who works in the

chemical laboratory at the hospital,' he said. 'He cannot find anyone to share the set of very pleasant rooms that he has found in Baker Street.'

'Then I am the man for him!' I cried. 'I should prefer sharing than living alone.'

Stamford looked at me strangely over his glass. 'You don't know Sherlock Holmes yet,' he said. 'Perhaps you would not care for him as a constant companion.'

'What is there against him?'

'Oh, nothing,' said Stamford

quickly. 'He is a little strange in his ideas, but a decent enough fellow. He knows a lot about chemistry and likes to gather a lot of trivial knowledge. I have no idea what his career plans are.'

'Have you ever asked him?'

Stamford shook his head. 'He is not a man who talks much about himself – or anything else for that matter.'

'I should like to meet him,' I said, eagerly. 'A quiet and studious man sounds just the sort I would prefer. I had enough noise and excitement in Afghanistan to last me a lifetime.'

'Then we shall drive to the laboratory after lunch,' said Stamford.

As we made our way to the hospital, Stamford told me a few more details about the man I was about to meet.

'Don't blame me if you don't get on with him,' said Stamford.

'I have only met him a few times in the laboratory.'

'If we don't get on it will be easy to part company,' I said. 'But it seems to me, Stamford,' I added, looking hard at him, 'that there must be a reason that you don't want to be held responsible. What is it? Tell me honestly.'

Stamford laughed. 'Holmes seems a little cold-blooded. I think that if he were conducting an experiment, he would not hesitate to try it out on a friend to see what happened. Not from an evil mind, you understand, but just out of curiosity – and he would try it out on himself too. He seems to have a passion for definite and exact knowledge.'

'Quite right too.'

'Yes, but that could be taken to excess.'

I mulled this over until we reached the hospital.

Chapter Two

'Here we are,' said my companion as we stepped out of the cab, 'you must judge for yourself.'

We turned into a narrow lane and entered through a small side door into the hospital. After winding our way through the building, we reached the chemical laboratory. Broad, low tables were covered with test tubes and Bunsen burners with flickering blue flames. Only one person was in the room, bending over a table absorbed in his work. All at once he sprang up with pleasure.

'I've found it! I've found it!' He ran towards us with a test tube in his hand. 'I have found a re-agent that reacts with the haemoglobin in blood!' His face shone with a delight that could not have been greater if he had struck gold.

'Dr Watson, Mr Sherlock Holmes,' said Stamford, introducing us.

'How are you?' The man gripped my hand with a strength I could hardly believe. 'You have been in Afghanistan, I perceive.'

'How on earth do you know that?' I asked, astonished.

'Never mind,' he said, chuckling to himself, 'but about the haemoglobin test. No doubt you see the significance?'

'Interesting, no doubt.'

Haemoglobin

A substance in blood that gives it its red colour. It carries oxygen from the lungs to every cell in the body. Blood with oxygen in it is bright red. Arteries carry this blood directly from the heart to all parts of the body, while veins carry blood back to the heart. By then it has given up most of its oxygen and become darker in colour.
To save life it is vital to know whether someone is bleeding from a vein or from an artery using this colour difference.

'Why, man, it is the most practical discovery for years. It gives us a reliable test for blood stains!'

He seized me by the coat sleeve and dragged me over to the table where he had been working.

'Let us have some fresh blood,' he said, digging a needle into his finger and drawing a drop of blood into a pipette. 'Now I add this blood to a litre of water. You see how it now looks like pure water? The blood is completely diluted.'

Into the mixture he threw some white crystals and added a few drops of a clear fluid. In an instant

the contents turned a reddish brown and then a brownish powder sank to the bottom of the glass jar.

'Ha!' he cried, clapping his hands like a small child with a new toy. 'What do you think of that?'

'It seems to be a very precise test,' I said.

'The old tests were clumsy and uncertain. Had this test been invented years ago, hundreds of men now walking the earth would have paid the penalty for their crimes.'

'Indeed,' I said.

'So many criminal cases hinge on the one point: are the brownish stains on the culprit's clothing from mud, rust, fruit … or blood? Now there is a reliable test: the Sherlock Holmes test.'

At this he put his hand on his heart and bowed as if to an imaginary audience.

'You are to be congratulated,' I said, surprised at his enthusiasm.

Yet I could, of course, see how useful such a test would be to the police.

Holmes gave me a gracious smile and put a plaster on the finger he had punctured. I could see that his hands were covered with similar pieces of plaster and discoloured by strong acids.

'We came here on business,' said Stamford, sitting down on a stool and pushing another towards me with his foot. 'My friend here is looking for lodgings and you were complaining that you had no one with whom to share yours. I thought I would bring you both together.'

Sherlock Holmes seemed delighted at the idea of sharing his rooms with me. 'I have my eye on some rooms in Baker Street,' he said, 'which would suit me perfectly. I generally have chemicals about and occasionally do experiments. Would that annoy you?'

‘Certainly not,’ I said, although privately feeling a little apprehensive.

‘Let me see,’ went on Mr Holmes, gazing into space. ‘What are my other faults? I get a bit depressed at times and don’t speak for days on end. You must not think I’m sulky when I do that. Just leave me alone and I’ll be all right. What about you? It’s just as well that we know the worst about each other before we begin to live together.’

‘Well, I object to loud noises because my nerves are shaken as a result of combat. I get up at all sorts of ungodly hours and I'm extremely lazy. I also still keep my old service revolver, though probably more from sentiment than for practical use. I have another set of vices when I'm well, but those are the ones at present.'

'Do you include violin playing in your set of annoyances?'

'It depends on the player,' I said. 'A well-played violin is a treat for the gods but a badly-played one ...'

'Oh, that's all right!' he cried with a merry laugh. 'I think we may consider it settled if the rooms are suitable for you. Call for me here at noon tomorrow and we'll go together and settle everything.'

We shook hands. Stamford and I left him working with his chemicals and walked together towards my hotel.

'By the way,' I asked suddenly, stopping and turning towards him. 'How on earth did he know that I came from Afghanistan?'

My companion smiled mysteriously. 'That's just his little

peculiarity,' he said. 'Many people wonder how he knows the things he does.'

'Oh, a mystery is it?' I rubbed my hands together in anticipation. 'I am much obliged to you for bringing us together. The study of a man interests me a good deal.'

'You'll find him a knotty problem,' said Stamford as he bade me goodbye. 'I'll bet he learns more about you than you do about him.'

We shook hands and I strolled into my hotel, giving much thought to my new acquaintance.

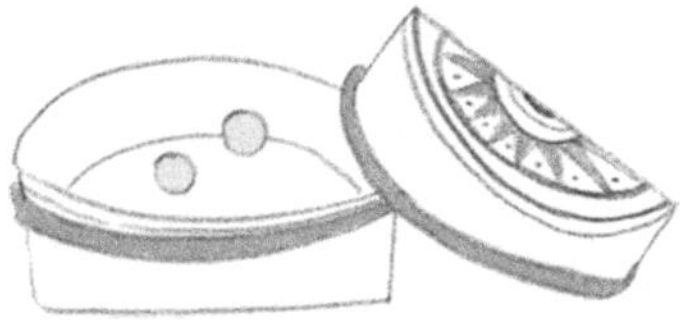

Chapter Three

The next day I met Sherlock Holmes as arranged and we went to see the rooms at 221B Baker Street. Two comfortable bedrooms and a large sitting room took up the first and second floors with two broad windows looking out onto Baker Street.

The cost was very reasonable, and we agreed on the spot to live there together. I returned

221B

to the hotel to collect my things and brought them over that very evening. Sherlock Holmes moved in the next morning with several boxes and suitcases, and we both began unpacking. I was delighted both with the lodgings and my fellow tenant.

Holmes was not a difficult man to live with. He was almost always in bed before ten at night and left the house before I got up in the morning. Often he worked at an almost feverish pace at the hospital, but as he had described, he sometimes seemed to fall into a kind of melancholy and spent days just lounging on the sofa hardly uttering a word.

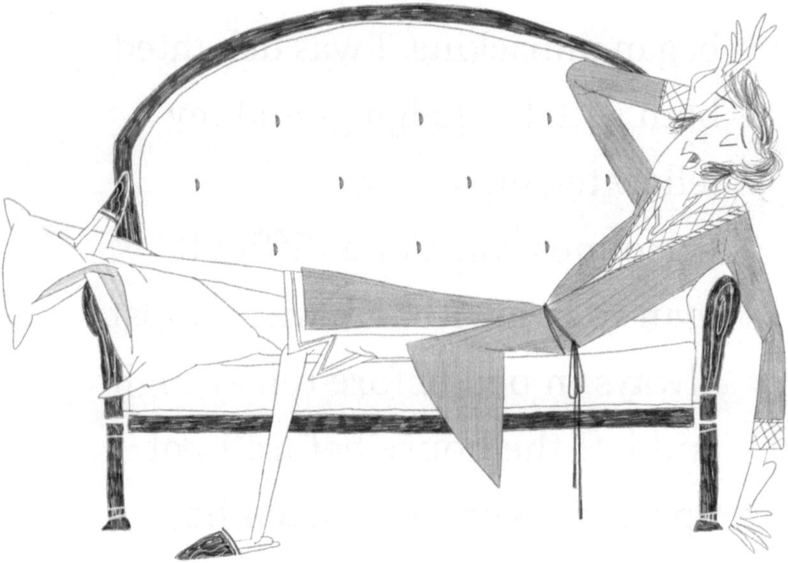

I became more and more intrigued by the man. His very

appearance and manner were unusual. He was the kind of person that caught people's attention, being over six feet tall and so slender that he appeared even taller. His eyes were piercing, and his chin and hawk-like nose made him look decisive and alert.

I had ample time to study Holmes because I was still not well enough to continue working as a doctor, nor even to venture out unless the weather was mild. I had no friends to call on me and so I enjoyed the mystery that hung around Holmes. I still did not know exactly what he did. He had enormous interest in some subjects but none in others. He knew many random facts, but none that would lead to any career. Of other more general knowledge he was ignorant. I discovered that he knew nothing of the solar system and I could not believe that, in the nineteenth century, there could be anyone who did not know that the earth revolved around the sun.

'You seem surprised,' he said. 'But now that I do know it, I shall do my best to forget it.'

'To forget it?'

'You see,' he explained, 'I believe that a man's brain is like an empty attic: you may stock it with whatever you choose, but it is not elastic, so you must choose wisely what you consider important.'

'But the solar system!' I protested.

'What good is that to me?' he said, impatiently. 'You say that we go around the sun. If we went around the moon it would not make a pennyworth of difference to me or my work.'

This would have been an opportunity to ask what his work was, but something in his expression stopped me. I did, however, decide to write down what I had so far discovered.

After I completed my list, I threw it into the fire in frustration. I wanted to know what occupation needed all of these accomplishments.

I have said that his violin playing was good, but like his temperament, it was erratic. He would play some difficult pieces that were most enjoyable, but when left to his own devices he would lean back in his

Sherlock Holmes

Knowledge

- Chemistry – extensive. Does a lot of experiments
- An expert on plant-based poisons but ignorant of gardening
- Can tell different soils and muds from each other
- Expert boxer and swordsman
- Knows a lot about human and animal anatomy
- Expert in British law and criminal history – knows every detail of every horror committed this century
- Plays violin well

Ignorance

- Literature
- Philosophy
- Astronomy
- Politics

chair and scrape aimlessly at the violin lying flat on his knee. Then there were no recognisable tunes, but they had definite moods as though he were voicing his thoughts through the music. They could be sad and melancholy or fantastic and cheerful. These could be trying to the listener, but he always made up for it by playing a number of my favourite pieces afterwards.

During the first week we had no callers, but then a number of people began to call, seemingly from all walks of life. There was a sallow, rat-faced little fellow introduced to me as Mr Lestrade, who came three or four times in one week. Another day a girl called. She was young and fashionably dressed and stayed for half an hour or so. That same afternoon a grey-haired, seedy-looking fellow came, and later a rather untidy elderly woman.

When any of these arrived, Holmes would apologise to me for the inconvenience, but ask that I stay in my bedroom during the visit. 'I have to use this room as my place of business,' he said, 'and these people are my clients.'

I was all the more intrigued.

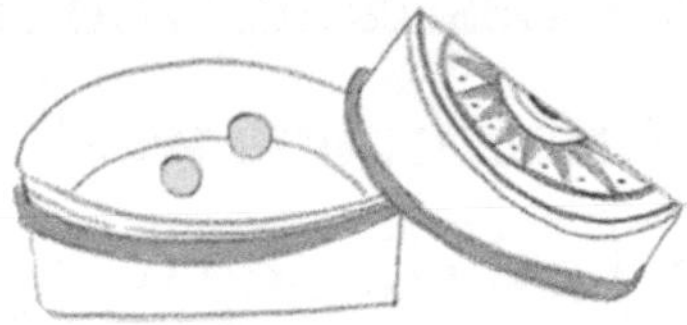

Chapter Four

One morning I got up earlier than usual and found Holmes still eating his breakfast. The landlady, Mrs Hudson, had not yet prepared my coffee so I rang the bell to call her. Then I picked up a magazine and began to browse through it as my companion chewed his toast.

One of the articles had a pencil mark beside it so naturally I began to read. It was rather ambitiously called 'The Book of Life'.

> An observant person may learn much by an accurate and systematic examination of all that comes his way.

The writer claimed to be able to read a person's innermost thoughts by a momentary expression, twitch of a muscle or glance of an eye; that no deceit or lie could pass unobserved to one trained in observation and analysis.

I sighed impatiently but continued to the end. The writer went on to say:

> The art of science and deduction requires long and patient study for which a lifetime is not long enough. Before looking at the aspects of a matter that are the most difficult, one should begin with the more elementary aspects. On meeting someone, one should learn to deduce the history of the man and his trade at a glance.

By his fingernails, coat sleeve, boots, trouser knees, hands and expression, one can tell his occupation.

'What absolute twaddle!' I cried, slapping the magazine down on the table. 'I never read such rubbish in all my life!'

'What is it?' asked Holmes.

'This article. I see you've read it because you have marked it. I don't deny that it's cleverly written, but it irritates me. It must be the theory of some armchair lounger since it is not practical. I would like to see him put into a third class carriage on the Underground and asked to give the occupations of his fellow travellers. I would bet against him being able to do so.'

'You would lose your money,' said Holmes, calmly. 'I wrote that article myself.'

'You!'

'Yes. I have a talent for both observation and deduction. These theories are extremely practical; so practical that I depend on them for my bread and cheese.'

‘And how?’ I asked.

At last I was to learn his occupation.

‘Well, I suppose I am the only one in the world. A consulting detective, that is. Here in London we have lots of government detectives and lots of private ones. When these fellows have a problem they come to me. They lay all the evidence before me and I am generally able, with the help of my knowledge of the history of crime, to set them straight. Lestrade is a well-known detective. He had a

problem recently, over a forgery case, and that was what brought him here.'

'And the other people?'

'They are all people who are in trouble and want a little help. I listen to their story, they listen to my comments, and then I pocket my fee.'

'So what you are saying is that, without leaving your room, you can unravel some knot that they cannot, yet they have seen every detail for themselves?'

'Quite so,' said Holmes. 'Now and again a case comes up that requires me to go and see things with my own eyes. You see, I have a lot of knowledge that I apply to the problem, and observation is second nature to me. You appeared surprised when I told you on our first meeting that you had come from Afghanistan.'

'You were told, no doubt.'

'Nothing of the sort. The knowledge that you came from Afghanistan came to me immediately. In a split second I thought, here is a gentleman of a medical type, but with the air of a military man. Clearly an army doctor then. He has just come from the tropics for his face is dark, and that is not the natural tint of his skin for his wrists are fair. He has undergone hardship and sickness as his haggard face clearly shows. His left arm has been injured because he holds it in a stiff and unnatural manner. Where in the tropics could an English army doctor have seen such hardship and got his arm wounded? Clearly in Afghanistan.'

'It is simple enough when you explain it,' I said with a smile.

I thought to myself that Holmes may be clever but he knew it too well. I walked to the window and looked out upon the street below.

'There are no crimes or criminals these days,' said Holmes. 'What use is it having brains? I know I have it in me to make my name famous for there's no one else who has put so much study into the detection of crime as I have. But what is the result? There is no crime that is not so simple that a Scotland Yard official can solve it.'

I was getting fed up with his arrogance so decided to change the subject.

'I wonder what that fellow is looking for?' I asked, pointing to a plainly dressed man walking slowly down the other side of the street and peering anxiously at the numbers on the doors. In his hand he held a large blue envelope. He was evidently the bearer of a message.

'You mean the retired sergeant of marines?' asked Holmes, having joined me at the window.

You bragger, I thought. *You know I cannot verify your guess.*

All at once the man spotted the number on our door, crossed the street, and then we heard a loud knock on the door, voices in the hall, and his heavy footsteps on the stairs.

The door opened. 'For Mr Sherlock Holmes,' said the man, stepping into the room and handing my friend a letter.

Here was my opportunity to teach Holmes a lesson. 'May I ask, my man, what your trade may be?'

'Commissionaire, sir,' he said, gruffly. 'Uniform away for repairs.'

Commissionaire

Trustworthy and true, these are usually retired or injured members of the armed forces who find employment as doormen or security officers. They are very loyal to their employers. Astute and observant, they make ideal witnesses.

‘And you were?’ I asked, with a slightly petty glance at Holmes.

‘A sergeant, sir, Royal Marine Light Infantry, sir. No answer, sir?’

He clicked his heels together, raised his hand in salute, and was gone.

I was amazed at this fresh proof of Holmes’ abilities, yet, in the back of my mind, I wondered whether it had been set up to impress me. I looked at him and I noticed that he had finished reading the note. His eyes had a vacant expression as though he were deep in thought.

‘How in the world did you deduce that?’ I asked.

'Deduce what?' He sounded irritated.

'That he was a retired sergeant of marines.'

'I have no time for trifles,' he said briskly, but then smiled. 'Excuse my rudeness, but you broke the thread of my thoughts. So you weren't able to see for yourself that he was a sergeant of marines?'

'No, indeed.'

'Even across the street I could see a great blue anchor tattooed on the back of one hand. That gave me the sea connection. He had the walk of a military man as well as the regulation side-whiskers. There we have the marine. He was a man with some amount of self-importance and an air of command. You must have noticed the way he held his head? A steady, respectable, middle-aged man – all facts that led me to believe he was a sergeant.'

'Wonderful!' I exclaimed.

'Commonplace,' said Holmes, although I noticed by his expression that he was pleased at my surprise and admiration. 'Just now I said that there were no criminals but I was wrong, it seems. Just look at this!' He handed me the note the commissionaire had brought. 'Would you mind reading it aloud?'

'Gregson is the smartest police officer in Scotland Yard,' said Holmes. 'He and Lestrade are the pick of a bad lot. They are both energetic but extremely conventional. Neither has the ability to think beyond the limits of what they were taught. They are as jealous as a pair of beauty queens. There will be some fun in this case if both are engaged in it.'

My dear Mr Sherlock Holmes,
There has been a bad business during the night at 3, Lauriston Gardens, off the Brixton Road. An officer saw a light there at about two in the morning and, as the house is empty, suspected that something was wrong. He found the door open and in the front room was the body of a well-dressed gentleman. In his pocket was a business card with the name Enoch J. Drebber, Cleveland, Ohio, USA.

There had been no robbery nor is there any evidence to show how the man died. There is blood in the room but no wounds on his body. The whole thing is a puzzle. If you can come round any time before twelve, you will find me here. I have left everything as it is until I hear from you. If you are unable to come, I shall give you full details and would consider it a great kindness if you would give me your opinion.

Yours faithfully,
Tobias Gregson

'Surely there is not a moment to be lost,' I cried, amazed at his slowness to act. 'Shall I order a cab?'

'I'm not sure whether I shall go,' said Holmes, strolling over to a window and idly gazing out. 'I really am the laziest fellow, although I can be active if the situation demands it.'

'Surely this is just such a chance that you've been waiting for?'

'My dear fellow, what does it matter to me? If I unravel the whole mystery you can be sure that Gregson and Lestrade will take all the credit, since they are officials in the case.'

'But he begs you to help them.'

'Yes, he knows that I am his superior and will acknowledge it to me, but never to anyone else. However, we may as well go and have a look. I shall work it out in my own way and may have a laugh at them if nothing else. Come on!'

He hurried to put on his coat and bustled about showing that the energetic mood had overtaken the lazy one.

'Get your hat,' he said.

'You wish me to come?'

'Yes, if you have nothing better to do.'

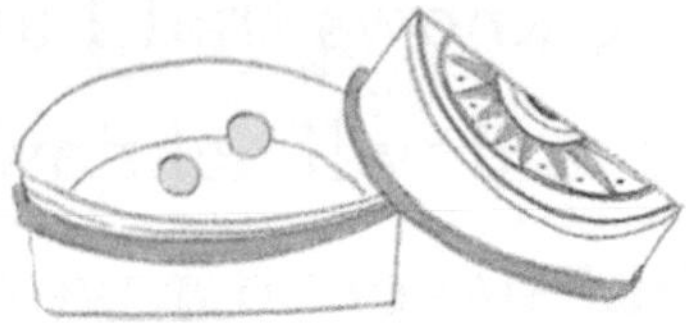

Chapter Five

A minute later we were both in a hansom cab driving furiously towards the Brixton Road. Holmes was in the best of spirits, prattling away about violins and the differences between them, but I was silent, feeling a little depressed both by the miserable weather and the sad business we were about to witness.

'You don't seem to be giving much thought to this case,' I said.

'It's a mistake to theorise before we have all the evidence. It biases the judgement.'

'You will have all the evidence soon,' I remarked, pointing. 'This is the Brixton Road and that is the house, if I'm not mistaken.'

'So it is. Stop, driver, stop!' We were still a hundred yards away but he insisted that we finish our journey on foot.

Number 3, Lauriston Gardens had a menacing look about it. It was one of four that stood back from the street; two occupied and two empty. The empty ones had blank windows except for the "To Let" signs pasted on them. The small front gardens were covered in weeds and each had a yellowish gravelly path, sloppy from the rain, leading up to the door. In the front, separating it from the footpath, was a three-foot brick wall with a fringe of wooden rails on top. Against this wall a police constable leaned, firmly keeping back the little knot of onlookers who craned their necks in the vain hope of catching a glimpse of what was happening in the house.

I imagined that Holmes would hasten into the house,

but instead he strolled up and down the pavement gazing vacantly at the ground, the sky, the houses opposite and the line of railings. Then, as I watched curiously, he walked slowly up the path, keeping his eyes riveted to the ground. Twice he stopped and once I saw him smile and exclaim in satisfaction. There were many footprints in the wet soil and since the police had been coming and going, I could not imagine how there could be any significant marks for Holmes to see. Still, he had shown that he could deduce things that others couldn't and I had no doubt he had learnt something from his examinations.

At the door of the house we were met by a tall, white-faced blond man with a notebook in his hand. He rushed forwards and vigorously shook Holmes' hand. 'It is kind of you to come,' he said. 'I have had everything left untouched.'

'Except that,' my friend said, pointing to the pathway. 'If a herd of buffalo had passed along it there could not be a greater mess. No doubt, however, you had drawn your own conclusions before you allowed it, Gregson.'

'I have had so much to do in the house that I left this to Lestrade.'

Holmes glanced at me and raised his eyebrows sardonically.

'With two such men as you and Lestrade, there will be little for me to discover,' he said.

Gregson rubbed his hands. 'I think we have done all that can be done,' he said in a self-satisfied way.

'You did not come here in a cab?' Holmes asked suddenly.

'No, sir.'

'Nor Lestrade?'

'No, sir.'

'Then let us go and look at the room.'

He strode into the house followed by Gregson. I pondered the seemingly irrelevant question he had asked before stepping through the front door myself.

The short passage, which led through to the kitchen, had doors leading off to left and right. One was closed but the other hung open, revealing the dining room where the mysterious affair had occurred. Holmes and Gregson walked in confidently but I followed somewhat reluctantly, knowing what lay inside.

It was a large square room empty of furniture. The walls were covered with vulgar large-patterned wallpaper blotched in places with mildew. Here and there strips had become detached and hung down exposing the yellow plaster beneath. Opposite the door was a showy fireplace, with the stump of a red wax candle on top. The solitary window was so dirty that the light was hazy, giving a dull grey tinge to everything, which was intensified by the thick layer of dust coating the whole room.

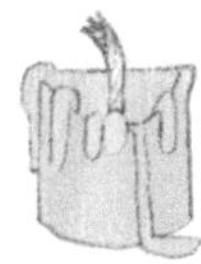

All these details I saw at a glance and only recalled later. My attention was focussed on the single motionless figure that lay stretched upon the floorboards. It was a man in his mid-forties with curly black hair and a short, stubbly beard. He was dressed in a heavy frock-coat, a waistcoat and light-coloured trousers. Beside him on the floor lay a well-brushed top hat.

The man's hands were clenched and his arms thrown out sideways while his legs were crossed at the ankles. His face held an expression of both horror and hatred exaggerated by his low forehead and protruding jaw, giving him an ape-like appearance.

I had never seen so fearsome a sight, made all the worse by the dark, grimy house.

Lestrade, lean and ferret-like as ever, stood by the doorway and greeted us.

'This case will make a stir, sir,' he remarked. 'It beats anything I have ever seen.'

'There is no clue?' asked Gregson.

'None at all,' said Lestrade.

Sherlock Holmes approached the body and, kneeling down, examined it intently. 'You are sure there is no wound?' he asked, pointing to the splashes of blood that lay all around.

'Positive!' cried both detectives.

'Then this blood must belong to another person – presumably the murderer, if a murder has been committed.'

As he spoke his nimble fingers were flying here and there, feeling, pressing, unbuttoning and examining; while his eyes wore the familiar faraway expression. The examination was made so quickly one could barely realise how thorough it was. Finally he bent forwards and sniffed the man's lips and then glanced at the solcs of his leather boots.

'He has not been moved at all?'

'No more than was necessary for the examination.'

'Then I am finished,' said Holmes, standing up.

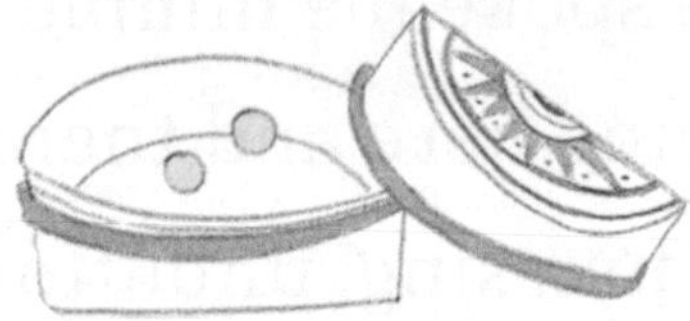

Chapter Six

At Gregson's command, four men with a stretcher came in and lifted the body onto it. As they did a ring tinkled down and rolled across the floor. Lestrade grabbed it and stared, mystified.

'There's been a woman here. It's a woman's wedding ring.' As he spoke he held it out in the palm of his hand. We all gathered round and gazed at it.

'This complicates matters,' said Gregson, 'as if they weren't complicated enough before.'

'Are you sure it doesn't simplify them?' asked Holmes. 'There's nothing to be learned by staring at it. What did you find in his pockets?'

'We have it all here,' said Gregson. He led us to a pile of objects on one of the bottom steps of the stairs, most of which was jewellery. 'The most interesting is this Russian leather card case, with cards of Enoch J. Drebber of Cleveland,

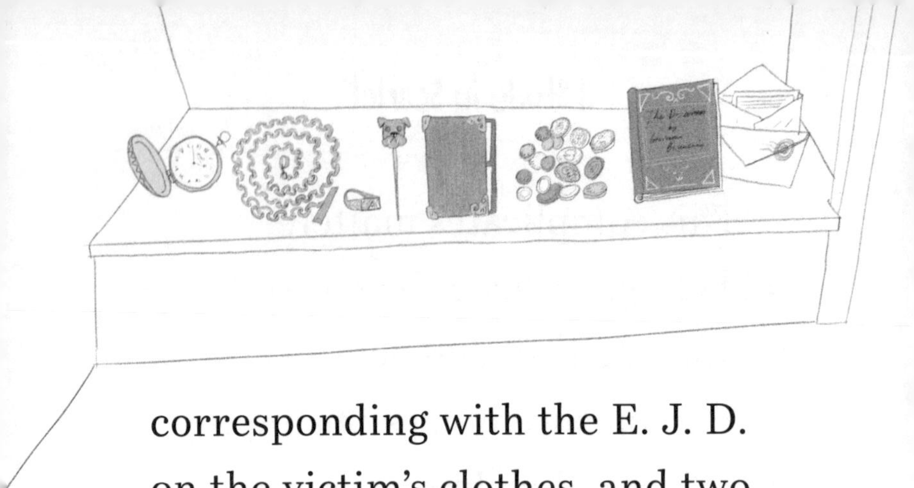

corresponding with the E. J. D. on the victim's clothes, and two letters – one addressed to E. J. Drebber and one to Joseph Stangerson.'

'At what address?'

'American Exchange, Strand. They are both from the Guion Steamship Company, and refer to the sailing of their boats from Liverpool. It is clear that the unfortunate man was about to return to New York.'

'Have you made any enquiries about this Stangerson fellow?'

'I did it at once, sir,' said Gregson. 'I have put advertisements in all the newspapers, and one of my men has gone to the American Exchange, but has not returned yet.'

'Have you contacted Cleveland?'

'We sent a telegram this morning.'

'How did you word your enquiries?'

'We simply explained what had happened, and said that we should be glad of any information.'

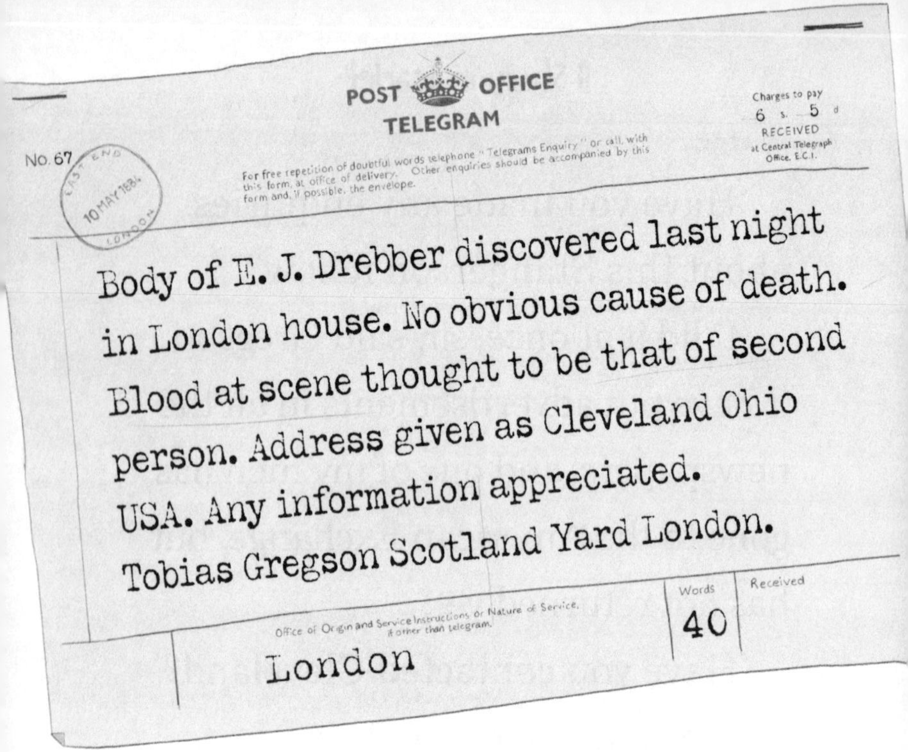
POST OFFICE
TELEGRAM

No. 67

EAST END 10 MAY 1881 LONDON

For free repetition of doubtful words telephone "Telegrams Enquiry" or call, with this form, at office of delivery. Other enquiries should be accompanied by this form and, if possible, the envelope.

Charges to pay 6 s. 5 d
RECEIVED
at Central Telegraph Office, E.C.I.

Body of E. J. Drebber discovered last night in London house. No obvious cause of death. Blood at scene thought to be that of second person. Address given as Cleveland Ohio USA. Any information appreciated.
Tobias Gregson Scotland Yard London.

Office of Origin and Service Instructions or Nature of Service, if other than telegram.
London

Words 40

Received

Holmes chuckled as he read Gregson's message. He appeared about to say something further when Lestrade, who had been in the front room while we were in the hall, came out rubbing his hands in a self-satisfied manner.

'Mr Gregson,' he said, 'I have just made a discovery of the highest importance, and one that would have been overlooked had I not made a careful examination of the walls.'

The little man's eyes sparkled as he spoke. I could see that he

Telegraphy

The fastest means of communication. Messages are sent electrically and delivered in minutes, but must be short as they are charged by the word. Unfortunately they are open for anyone to read, and risk falling into the wrong hands. For this reason it can be a good idea to use code. Messages must be sent from one telegraph office to another.

was smug at having scored a point against his colleague.

'Come here,' he said, bustling back into the room. He struck a match and held it up against the wall.

'Look at that!'

In this corner of the room a large piece of wallpaper had peeled away exposing a yellow square of plastering. Across this bare space, scrawled in blood-red letters, was a single word:

RACHE

'What do you think of that?' cried the detective. 'This was overlooked because it was the

darkest corner of the room and no one thought of looking here. The murderer has written it with his or her own blood. This proves that it wasn't suicide. Why was this corner chosen? I'll tell you. See that candle on the mantelpiece? It was lit at the time, so this corner would have been the brightest, not the darkest portion of the wall.'

'And what does it mean, now that you have found it?' asked Gregson. I noticed the hint of a sneer in his voice.

'Mean? Why it means that the murderer was going to write the name Rachel, but was disturbed before they had time to finish. Mark my words, before this case is solved you will find that a woman named Rachel has something to do with it. It's all very well for you to laugh, Mr Sherlock Holmes. You may be very clever, but the old hound is the best, when all is said and done.'

'I really beg your pardon,' said my companion, who had obviously ruffled Lestrade's temper by bursting into an explosion of laughter. 'You certainly take the credit for being the first to discover this and, as you say, it would seem to have been written by the other participant in tonight's mystery. I have not had time to examine this room yet, so with your permission I shall do so now.'

As he spoke he whipped a tape measure and a magnifying glass from his pocket and strode noiselessly about the room, sometimes stopping or kneeling, and once lying flat on his face. All the while he chattered away to himself as though he'd forgotten our presence. He let out exclamations, groans, and little cries of hope. As I watched him he reminded me of a well-trained bloodhound as it dashes backwards and forwards until it comes across the scent.

For twenty minutes he was engaged in his searches, measuring

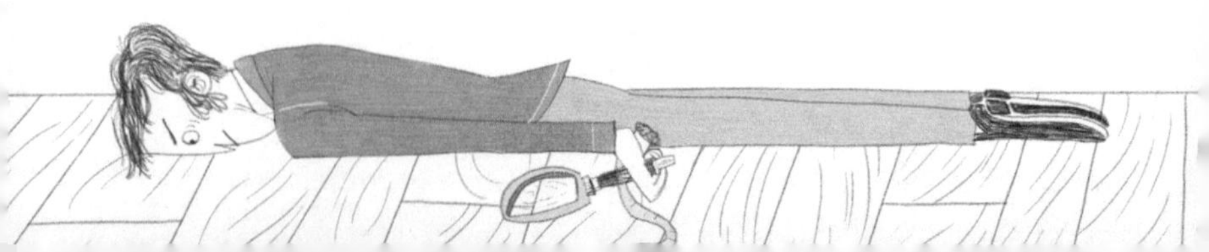

with exact care marks that were invisible to me. In one place he carefully gathered up a little pile of grey dust from the floor and placed it into an envelope. Finally, he examined the word on the wall with his magnifying glass, going over every letter slowly. Seeming satisfied at last, he put the tape measure and magnifying glass back into his pocket.

Gregson and Lestrade watched the movements of their amateur colleague with considerable curiosity and some contempt, I thought. They evidently failed to appreciate the fact, which I had begun to realise, that Sherlock Holmes' smallest actions were all directed towards some definite and practical end.

'What do you think of it, sir?' they both asked.

'You are doing so well now that it would be a pity for anyone to interfere and take away your credit.' There was sarcasm in his voice, which made me smile inwardly.

I was finding my new friend an interesting person to observe, and certainly an entertaining one.

'I should like to speak to the constable who found the body. Can you give me his name and address?'

'He's off duty now,' said Lestrade, turning to a page toward the front of his notebook and passing it over to Holmes.

John Rance, 46 Audley Court, Kensington Park Gate.

'Come along, Doctor,' said Holmes when he had made a note of the address, 'we shall go and look him up. I'll tell you one thing that may help you in the case,' he continued, turning to the two detectives. 'The murderer was a man. He was over six feet tall, was in the prime of life, had small feet for his height, wore coarse, square-toed boots, and smoked a Trichinopoly cigar. He came here with his victim in a four-wheeled cab, which was drawn by a horse with three old shoes and one new one. In all probability, the murderer had a red face and the fingernails of his right hand were very long. These are only a few indications, but they may help you.'

It was amusing to see the incredulous looks on the faces of Lestrade and Gregson.

'If this man was murdered, how was it done?' asked Lestrade.

'Poison,' said Holmes, curtly, and strode off. 'One more thing, Lestrade,' he added, turning round at the door. '"Rache" is the German word for "revenge", so don't lose time looking for Miss Rachel.'

This last piece of information was fired like a shot and left the two rival detectives open-mouthed.

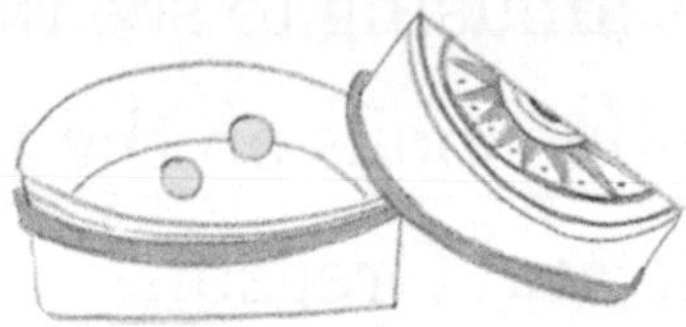

Chapter Seven

It was one o'clock when we left Lauriston Gardens. We then went to the telegraph office where Holmes sent a long telegram. Then we hailed a cab and ordered the driver to take us to the address Lestrade had given us.

'There is nothing like first-hand evidence,' he said as we clattered along the street. 'My mind is made up on the case, but we may as well learn all that is to be learned.'

'You amaze me, Holmes,' I said. 'Surely you are not as sure as you pretend to be about those particulars you gave?'

'Watson,' he said, turning to me. 'The first thing I noticed on arriving at the house was that a cab had made two ruts with its wheels close to the kerb. Now, until last night we have had no rain for a week so those marks must have been made during the night.'

I nodded. That was true enough.

'There were marks of the horses' hooves too,' he went on,

'and the outline of one was more clearly cut than the other three, showing that it was a new shoe. Since the cab was there after the rain yet neither detective came by cab, it must have been there during the night and brought those two men to the house.'

'But how about the other man's height?'

'In most cases a man's height can be told from the length of his stride. I noted this fellow's stride both outside in the clay and in the dust inside the house. Also, when a man writes on the wall, he tends to write just above the level of his eyes. That writing was just over six feet from the ground. It was child's play.'

'And his age?'

'Well, if a man can stride four and a half feet without any effort, he must still be in the prime of life. That was the width of a puddle on the path that he had crossed; Leather-boots had gone round it and but Square-toes had hopped straight over. There is no mystery about it at

all. I am simply applying a few of the rules of observation and deduction that I suggested in the article. Is there anything else that puzzles you?'

Now I could see the reason for all his foraging and close examination at the scene, although I knew that any observations of my own would not have led to the same conclusions.

'Well, what of the fingernails and the Trichinopoly cigar?'

'The writing on the wall was done with a man's forefinger

dipped in blood. Through my magnifying glass I could see that the plaster was slightly scratched showing that that nail, at least, was long. The cigar ash I gathered up from the floor. It was dark in colour and flaky – such an ash is only made by a Trichinopoly. I have made a study of cigar ash, Watson, and written a paper on the subject.'

I passed my hand over my brow. 'My head is in a whirl,' I said. 'The more I think about it, the more mysterious it grows.

Why did these two men come to an empty house? Where is the cabman who drove them there? Where did the blood come from? What was the motive for the murder, since it wasn't robbery? Why was a woman's ring there? And above all, why should the second man write the German word RACHE before leaving? I cannot see any way of explaining these facts.'

Holmes smiled approvingly. 'You sum up the facts well,' he said. 'There are still some things to explain, although I have made up my mind about the main facts. The word written on the wall was just a way of diverting the enquiry. It was not written by a German, since it did not fit the way a German would write the letters. I am not going to tell you much more of the case, Watson. If I tell you too much of my method of working, you will think that I am a very ordinary person after all.'

I smiled. 'I shall never do that. You have brought detection as near to an exact science as it ever will be.'

'I'll tell you one other thing,' he said. 'Leather-boots and Square-toes arrived together in the cab, and walked up the path together. When they got inside, Leather -boots stood still while Square-toes walked up and down, growing more and more excited. I could tell that by the length of his stride in the dust. He was talking all the while, working himself up into a fury. Then the tragedy occurred. Now I have told you all I know. We must hurry, for I want to go Halle's concert and hear Wilma

Norman-Neruda this afternoon. She plays exquisite violin.'

During this conversation our cab had been threading its way through dingy streets to stop at last in the dingiest of all. 'That's Audley Court in there,' said the driver, pointing to a narrow alley in the dead-coloured brick. 'You'll find me here when you come back.'

We picked our way through groups of ragged, dirty children who watched us curiously, ducked under lines of discoloured washing, and eventually came to Number 46. On the door was a small brass plate with the name Rance engraved on it.

Holmes knocked, and a dark-haired woman opened the door, wiping her hands on her apron.

'We should like to speak to Constable Rance,' said Holmes.

The woman glanced behind her up some stairs. 'He's asleep, sir, but if it's important I'll wake him.' She showed us into a little front parlour.

Rance appeared looking a little cross at being disturbed. 'I made my report at the office,' he said. 'If it's about the body.'

Holmes took a half-sovereign from his pocket and toyed with it, deep in thought. 'We thought that we should like to hear it from your own lips,' he said.

'I should be most happy to tell you anything I can,' the constable answered, keeping his eyes on the gold coin.

'Just tell it in your own way.'

'I'll tell you from the beginnin',' he said. 'My shift is from ten at night until six in the morning. Apart from a fight at the White Hart at eleven, it was a quiet night. At one o'clock it began to rain and I met a colleague, Murcher, and we stood together at the corner of Henrietta Street, talkin'. Just after two o'clock I thought I would take a look to see if all was right down the Brixton Road. It was very lonely an' I never met a soul, though a cab or two went past me. I was just thinking how well a hot drink would go down when suddenly the glint of a light caught my eye in a window. Now, I knew

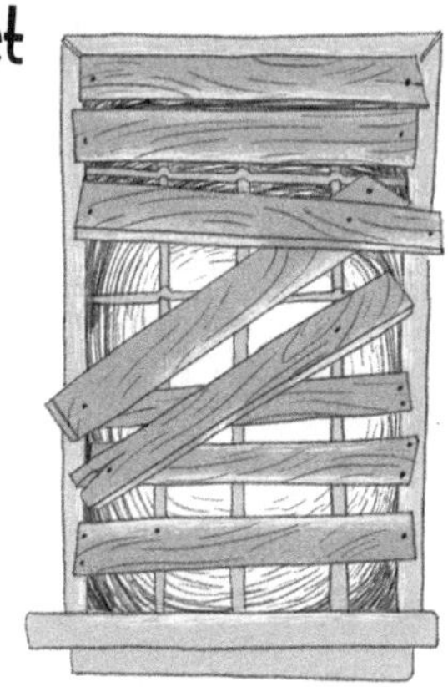

those two houses in Lauriston Avenue were empty on account of the owner not fixin' the drains. The last tenant what lived in one of them died of typhoid fever. I was surprised at seeing a light in the window and suspected somethin' was wrong. When I got to the door–'

'You stopped, and then walked back

to the gate,' my companion interrupted. 'What did you do that for?'

Rance jumped and stared at Holmes with utter amazement on his face. 'Why, that's true, sir,' he said, 'though how you come to know it, heaven knows. You see, when I got to the door it was so still and lonely that I thought it best to have someone with me. I'm not afraid of much but thought it might be the ghost of the fellow what died of typhoid. I looked to see if I could see Murcher, but there wasn't no sign of him, nor anyone else.'

'There was no one in the street?'

'Not a soul, sir. Then I went back and pushed the door open. All was quiet inside so I went into the room where the light was burnin'. There was a candle flickerin' on the mantelpiece and by its light I saw–'

'Yes, I know what you saw. You walked round the room several times, and you knelt down by the body, and then you walked through and tried the kitchen door, and then–'

John Rance sprang to his feet with a frightened look on his face and suspicion in his eyes. 'Where was you hid to see all that?' he cried. 'It seems to me that you knows a great deal more than you should.'

Holmes laughed and threw his personal card across the table.

'I am not the murderer,' he said. 'I'm one of the hounds, not the wolf. Mr Lestrade and Mr Gregson will answer for that. What did you do next?'

Rance sat down again, still looking mystified, and I sympathised with him. 'I went back to the gate and blew my whistle. That brought Murcher and two more.'

'Was the street empty then?'

'Well, as far as anybody that could be of use.'

'What do you mean?'

The constable grinned. 'I've seen many a drunk chap in my time but never any as far gone as that fellow. He couldn't stand, far less help. We'd have taken him to the station if we hadn't been so occupied.'

'Did you notice his face? His dress?'

broke in Holmes, impatiently.

'I should think I did, since I had to prop him up – me and Murcher between us. He was a tall chap with a red face, the lower part hidden by a scarf–'

'That will do,' said Holmes. 'What became of him?'

'We'd enough to do without lookin' after him. I'll bet he found

his way home all right.'

'How was he dressed?'

'A brown coat.'

'Had he a whip in his hand?'

'A whip? No.'

'He must have left it behind,' muttered Holmes. 'You didn't hear or see a cab after that?'

Rance shook his head. 'No.'

'Here's a half-sovereign for you,' my companion said, standing up and taking his hat. 'I'm afraid you will never rise in the ranks, Rance. The man you held in your hands is the one we are seeking. Come along, Doctor.'

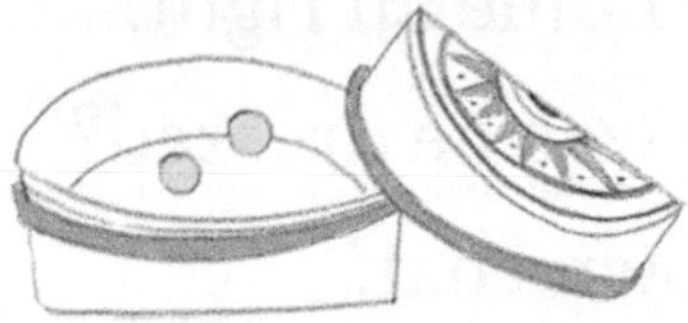

Chapter Eight

We returned to the cab, leaving the constable incredulous.

'The blundering fool!' said Holmes, bitterly, as we drove back to our lodgings. 'Just think of his having such a stroke of luck and not taking advantage of it.'

'I'm afraid it's a mystery to me too,' I admitted. 'It's true that the description of the man matches your idea of the second man, but why should he come back to the house after leaving it?'

'The ring, man, the ring. That was what he came back for. If we have no other way of catching him, we can always bait our line with the ring. I shall have him, Doctor, and I have you to thank. I might not have gone but for you, and missed the finest study I have come across. A study in scarlet, perhaps? After all, there's a scarlet thread of murder running

through the tapestry of life and we must expose it. And now for lunch and then the concert. Norman-Neruda's playing is splendid. What's that little thing of Chopin's she plays so magnificently? Tra la la.'

Leaning back in the cab, Holmes sang like a lark while I tried to fathom the many sides of the human mind.

After Holmes left for the concert I lay down on the sofa for a couple of hours' sleep. The morning had been tiring and I was still not completely well.

Still, it was a useless attempt.

My mind was full of Holmes' actions and deductions. I remembered how he had sniffed the man's lips. No doubt he had detected something that made him suggest poison. Other than that, there were no marks on the body, yet a lot of blood. No weapon nor any sign of a struggle.

Holmes was late returning – and I knew that the concert would not have lasted so long. Dinner was on the table before he appeared.

'It was magnificent!' he said, taking his seat. He looked at me more closely. 'What's the matter? Did the Brixton Road affair upset you?'

'To tell the truth, it has,' I said. 'You would think I would be more hardened to it after my experiences in Afghanistan.'

'I can understand. The mystery about this stimulates the imagination. Have you seen the evening paper?'

'No.'

'It gives a good account of the affair although it does not mention the ring, which is just as well.'

'Why?'

'Look at this advertisement,' he said. 'I had one sent to every paper this morning.'

He threw the paper across to me and I glanced at the place indicated. It was the first announcement in the "Found" column.

In Brixton Road this morning, a plain gold wedding ring found in the roadway between the White Hart tavern and Holland Grove. Apply Dr Watson, 221B Baker Street, between eight and nine this evening.

17

The Evening Standard

'Excuse me using your name,' he said. 'If I'd used my own, someone would have recognised it.'

'That's all right,' I said, 'but I have no ring.'

'Oh, yes you have,' he said, handing me one. 'This will do very well.'

'And who do you expect will answer this advertisement?'

'Why, the man in the brown coat – our red-faced friend with square toes. If he does not come himself, he will send an accomplice.'

'Would he not consider it too dangerous?'

'Not at all. I think this man would risk anything rather than lose the ring. I believe that he dropped it while stooping over Drebber's body. After leaving the house he discovered his loss. He hurried back but found the police there so he pretended to be drunk to avoid suspicions as to what he was doing out that time of night. He may think that he dropped the ring in the road so would look in the papers to see if it was found. Why should he fear a trap? He would see no reason why finding a ring should be anything to do with the murder. He will come. You shall see him within the hour.'

'And then?'

'Oh, you can leave me to deal with him then. Did you say you had a gun?'

'Yes, my service revolver.'

'You'd better clean it and load it. It is as well to be ready for anything.'

I went to my room and did as he suggested. When I returned with the gun, Holmes was engaged in his favourite occupation of scraping on the violin.

'The plot thickens,' he said as I entered. 'I have just had a reply to my American telegram. My view of the case is correct. Put your gun in your pocket. When the fellow comes, speak to him in a normal way. Leave the rest to me.'

'It's eight o'clock now,' I said, taking out my pocket watch and flicking it open.

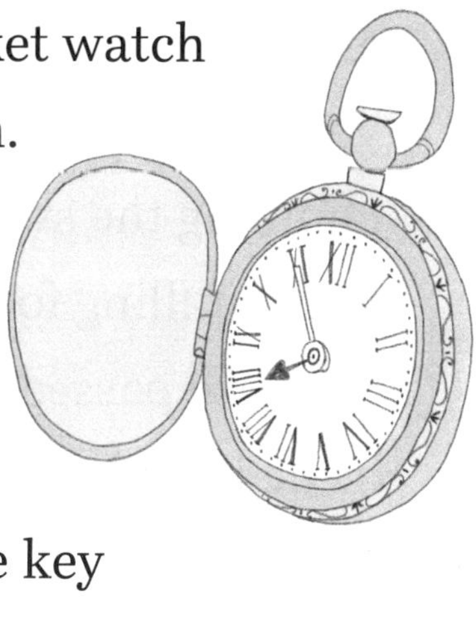

'Yes. He will probably be here in a few minutes. Open the door slightly and put the key on the inside.'

As he spoke there was a sharp ring on the doorbell. Holmes rose softly and moved his chair to face the door. We heard Mrs Hudson cross the hall and open the door. I found that I was holding my breath in anticipation.

'Does Doctor Watson live here?' asked a clear but rather harsh voice. Then we heard the person climbing the stairs with uncertain and shuffling footsteps. A look of surprise passed over Holmes' face as he listened.

There was a feeble tap at the door.

'Come in,' I cried.

Instead of the man of violence we were expecting, a very old and wrinkled woman hobbled into the room. She dropped a curtsy then stood blinking at us with bleary eyes, fumbling in her pocket with shaky fingers.

I glanced at Holmes and he had such a gloomy expression that it was all I could do to keep my face straight.

The old lady drew out an evening paper and pointed at our advertisement. 'It's this as has brought me, good gentlemen,' she said. 'A gold wedding ring in the Brixton Road. It belongs to my girl, Sally, as was married this time a year ago. Her husband is a sailor, and if he comes home and finds her without the ring, it's more than her life's worth. He's bad enough at the best of times and worse after a drink. She went to the circus last night along with–'

'Is this her ring?' I interrupted.

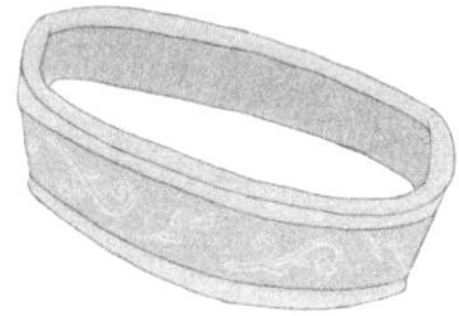

'The Lord be thanked,' cried the woman. 'Sally will be glad this night. That's the ring.'

'And what's your address?' I asked, picking up a pencil.

'13, Duncan Street, Houndsditch. Quite a way from here.'

'The Brixton Road does not lie between any circus and Houndsditch,' said Holmes, sharply.

The old woman turned and looked at him. 'The gentleman asked for my address. Sally lives in lodgings at 3, Mayfield Place, Peckham.'

'And your name is?'

'My name is Sawyer – hers is Dennis. Tom Dennis married her, and a smart, clean lad too, as long as he's at sea–'

'Here's your ring, Mrs Sawyer,' I interrupted at a sign from Holmes. 'I am glad to be able to restore it to its rightful owner.'

With many mumbled blessings and words of gratitude, the old lady put it in her pocket and shuffled down the stairs.

Holmes sprang to his feet the moment she had gone and disappeared into his bedroom, reappearing with his coat and scarf on. 'I'll follow,' he said. 'She must be an accomplice and will lead me to him. Wait up for me.'

Looking through the window, I watched her shuffle along the street with her pursuer remaining some distance behind. There was no need for Holmes to ask me to wait up. Sleep would be impossible until I heard the result of the adventure.

Instead I settled down to read a book.

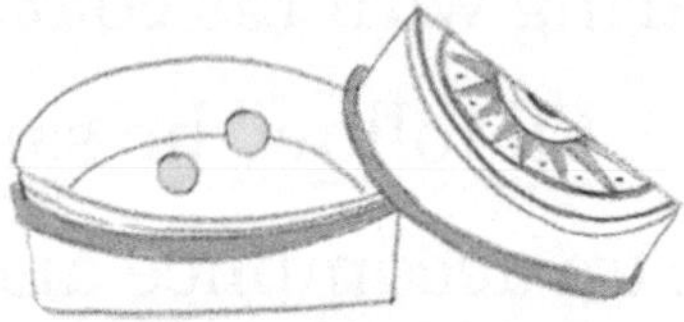

Chapter Nine

Time passed and at last, just before twelve, I heard his key in the door. The instant he entered the room I knew that he had not been successful. The expression on his face flickered between amusement and annoyance, but finally he burst into a hearty laugh.

'I wouldn't have those from Scotland Yard hear of this for the world!' he said. 'I would never hear the end of it.'

'What happened?'

'Oh, I don't mind telling a story against myself. The woman began to limp and hailed a four-wheeler cab that was passing. She gave the driver the address in such a loud voice that the whole street must have heard.

"Drive to 13, Duncan Street, Houndsditch," she cried. When she was inside I jumped onto the back of the cab – that's an art every detective should be expert at – and off we rattled. When we reached Duncan Street I jumped off before the cab stopped, the driver jumped down and opened the door, but no one got off. The driver was furious seeing no sign of his passenger or fare. I enquired at Number 13 but they had never heard of anyone called Sawyer or Dennis.'

I couldn't help but smile. 'You mean that feeble old woman was able to get out of a moving carriage without either you or the driver seeing her?'

'Old woman be damned!' said Holmes, sharply. 'We were certainly taken in. It must have been a very agile young man with a talent for acting. He knew that he was being followed and gave me the slip.'

I was suddenly very tired and I left Holmes seated in front of the fire when I went to bed, but late into the night I heard the wailings of his violin and knew that he was still pondering the strange problem that he had set himself to unravel.

The papers the next day were full of the "Brixton Mystery" as they called it.

Holmes and I read these articles together at breakfast, and they appeared to cause him great amusement.

The Daily News

10th May 1884

there is no doubt that this crime was a political one. Every effort must be made to find the secretary, Mr Stangerson, to understand the habits of the deceased. A great step has been gained by the discovery of the address of the house at which he boarded – a result that was entirely due to the acuteness and energy of Mr Gregson of Scotland Yard.

ENING STANDARD

10th May 1884

Lawless outrages of this sort usually occur under an unstable government, leading to weakening of authority …

We are glad to learn that Mr Lestrade and Mr Gregson, of Scotland Yard, are both engaged upon the case, and it is confidently anticipated that these astute officers will speedily throw light upon the matter.

'I told you that Lestrade and Gregson would get the credit.'

'It depends on how it turns out.'

'It doesn't matter in the least,' replied Holmes. 'If the man is caught it will be because of their efforts, and if he escapes, it will be in spite of their efforts.'

At that moment there came the pattering of many feet in the hall and on the stairs, accompanied by shouts from Mrs Hudson.

'What is it?' I cried.

'It's the Baker Street division of the detective police force,' said my companion, and as he spoke the door was flung open and in rushed half a dozen of the dirtiest and most ragged children I had ever seen.

'Attention!' cried Holmes, sharply, and the six little scoundrels stood in line like statues. 'In future you shall send up Wiggins alone to report. Have you found it, Wiggins?'

'No, sir, we ain't,' said one of the boys.

'I hardly expected you would. You must keep on until you do. Here are your wages.' He handed each of them a shilling. 'Now, off you go, and come back with a better report next time.'

He waved his hand and they scampered away downstairs. The next moment we heard their shrill voices in the street.

'There's more work to be got out of one of those little lads than out of a dozen of the force,' Holmes remarked. 'The mere sight of an official-looking person seals men's lips. These youngsters, however, go everywhere and hear everything. They are as sharp as needles too.'

'Is it on this Brixton case that you are employing them?'
I asked.

'Yes, there is a point that I wish to clarify. It is merely a matter of time,' he said, mysteriously. 'We are going to hear some news now! Here is Gregson coming down the road with a smug expression on his face. Yes, he's stopping!'

There was a violent ring of the doorbell and a few seconds later Gregson burst into our sitting room.

'My dear fellow,' he cried, wringing Holmes' hand. 'Congratulate me! I have made the whole thing as clear as day!'

A slight expression of anxiety crossed Holmes' face. 'Do you mean you are on the right track?'

'The right track! Why, sir, we have the man under lock and key.'

'And his name is?'

'Arthur Charpentier, sub-lieutenant in Her Majesty's

Navy,' cried Gregson, pompously rubbing his fat hands and puffing out his chest.

Holmes gave a sigh of relief and relaxed into a smile. 'Take a seat. We are anxious to know how you managed it. Will you have a drink with us?'

'I don't mind if I do,' the detective answered. 'The tremendous exertions I have gone through during the past couple of days have worn me out. Mental exertions too. You will appreciate that, Mr Sherlock Holmes, for we are both brain-workers.'

'You do me too much honour,' said Holmes. 'Let us hear how you arrived at this result.'

The detective seated himself in the armchair and sipped his drink. Then he suddenly slapped his thigh in amusement. 'The fun of it is,' he said, 'that fool Lestrade, who thinks himself so smart, has gone off upon the wrong track altogether. He is after the secretary,

Stangerson, who had nothing to do with the crime whatsoever.'

The idea tickled Gregson so much that he laughed until he nearly choked.

'And how did you get your clue?'

Gregson looked at me. 'Of course, Dr Watson, this is strictly between us. The first difficulty was finding the victim's relatives in America. I couldn't wait for a reply from my advertisements. You remember the hat beside the dead man?'

'Yes,' said Holmes, 'by John Underwood and Sons, 129 Camberwell Road.'

Gregson looked deflated. 'I had no idea that you noticed that,' he said. 'Did you go there?'

'No.'

'Ha!' said Gregson, relieved. 'Well, I went to Underwood and he looked through his books and found the sale. It was to a Mr Drebber, residing at Charpentier's Boarding House, Torquay Terrace. Thus I got his address.'

'Smart, very smart,' murmured Holmes.

'I next called upon Madame Charpentier,' continued Gregson. 'She was very pale and

distressed. Her daughter was in the room too, a very fine-looking girl, but red about the eyes and her lips trembled as I spoke to her. I began to smell a rat. You know how it is, Mr Sherlock Holmes, when you come upon the right scent – a kind of thrill in your nerves.

'I asked if she had heard of the death of their boarder, Mr Enoch Drebber. She nodded, seeming unable to speak, and the girl burst into tears. It was obvious that they knew something. In answer to my question, Madame Charpentier told me that Drebber had left the house at eight o'clock. His secretary, Mr Stangerson, had said there were two trains and he was to catch the earlier one at nine-fifteen.

'I asked if that was the last they had seen of him and her face went red. It was several seconds before she could say yes. After a few moments the daughter spoke calmly, suggesting to her mother that they tell the truth: that they did see Mr Drebber again.'

Holmes and I were silent as we hung on Gregson's every word.

'The mother then turned to me,' he continued, 'and said she would tell me all. She explained that her agitation was not because she thought for a minute that her son had anything to do with the crime, but that it would certainly look that way. I told her that if her son was innocent he had nothing to fear.

'Mr Drebber had been with them for three weeks after travelling with his secretary, Mr Stangerson, all over the continent. Stangerson was a quiet, reserved man but his employer was just the opposite. He was always drunk by noon and his manners toward the servants were quite disgusting. It seems he acted the same way with the daughter and once actually seized her arm and embraced her. Madame Charpentier gave him notice to leave her boarding house. Drebber did so but soon returned, the worse for drink. He forced his way inside, saying that he had missed the train. Then he turned to the daughter,

Alice, and suggested she go with him back to America. Poor Alice apparently screamed, and at that moment her brother, Arthur, came into the room. Drebber ran for the door with Arthur on his heels. Arthur soon returned and stood in the doorway with a stick in his hand and said ...'

Gregson looked down at his notebook.

'He said, "I don't think that fine fellow will trouble us again. I will go after him and see where he goes." He grabbed his hat and went off and the next morning there was news of Drebber's mysterious death.'

Gregson looked up at us. 'So you see, gentlemen, that would point to him being guilty. Madame Charpentier said that her son must have returned much later, certainly after she retired at eleven. Since the son is in the navy he was easy to find and I arrested him immediately. He knew what it was about.'

'What is your theory then?' asked Holmes.

'That he followed Drebber as far as the Brixton Road where there was another fight. Drebber received a blow from the stick, in the stomach perhaps, that killed him without leaving a mark. The night was wet so no one was about and Charpentier dragged his body into the empty house. As to the candle, the blood, and the writing on the wall, they may be tricks to throw the police onto the wrong scent.'

'Well done!' said Holmes in an encouraging voice. 'We shall make something of you yet, Gregson.'

'I flatter myself that I have managed it rather neatly,' said

Gregson proudly. 'The young man made a statement saying that he followed Drebber for a short way and then Drebber took a cab to get away from him. Charpentier says he met an old shipmate and they took a long walk together. He couldn't supply the address of this sailor though. I think the whole thing fits together nicely, and it amuses me to think of Lestrade going off on the wrong scent. Why, by Jove, here is the man himself!'

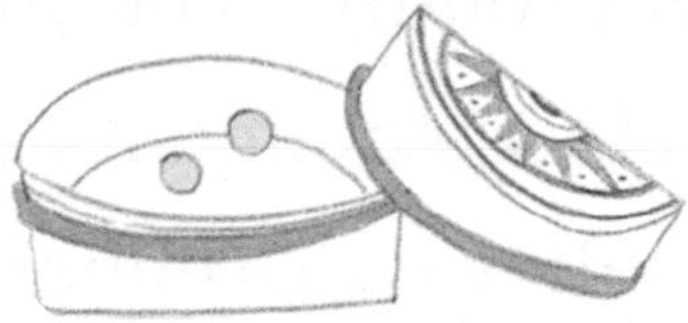

Chapter Ten

It was indeed a troubled-looking Lestrade who had entered while we were talking. He stood in the centre of the room looking embarrassed and fumbling with his hat.

'This is a most puzzling case,' he said.

'Ah, you find it so,' said Gregson, triumphantly.

'I thought you would come to that conclusion. Have you managed to find the secretary, Mr Joseph Stangerson?'

'The secretary, Mr Joseph Stangerson,' said Lestrade, gravely, 'was murdered at Halliday's Private Hotel at about six o'clock this morning.'

The information was so unexpected that we all three were dumbfounded. Gregson sprang out of his chair, spilling his drink. I stared in silence at Holmes, whose lips were compressed and brows drawn over his eyes. 'Stangerson too,' he muttered. 'The plot thickens.'

'Are you sure?' asked Gregson.

'I have just come from his room,' said Lestrade. 'I was the first to discover what had occurred. I was sure that Stangerson was concerned in the death of Drebber, but now see that I was mistaken. They were seen together at eight-thirty in the evening at Euston Station and then Drebber was found at two in the morning. I wanted to find out what Stangerson had been doing in the meantime. I telegraphed to Liverpool and asked them to watch the ships bound for America.

Then I set to work calling on all the hotels near Euston, thinking that Stangerson would have put up somewhere for the night before catching a train in the morning.'

'They must have agreed to meet somewhere beforehand,' said Holmes.

'So it proved. This morning I continued my search and finally reached the Halliday Private Hotel in Little George Street. They thought that I was the gentleman he was expecting and a young employee

showed me to his room on the second floor. He was just about to go downstairs again when I noticed something that made me feel sick, even after my twenty years' experience. From under the door curled a little red ribbon of blood. The lad nearly fainted when he saw it but together we put our shoulders to the door and knocked it in. The window was open and beside it, all huddled up, was the body of a man in night clothes. He had been stabbed in his left side. And now comes the strangest part. What do you suppose was above the murdered man?'

I felt a creeping of the flesh and a sense of horror as Holmes said, 'The word RACHE written in blood.'

'Just so,' said Lestrade.

There was something so cold and methodical about this crime that, despite being steady enough on the battlefield, my nerves now tingled as I thought of it.

'The murderer was seen,' went on Lestrade. 'A milk boy, passing on his way to the dairy early this

morning, noticed that a ladder was propped up against one of the windows on the second floor. After passing, he looked back and saw a man descend the ladder. He came down so openly that the lad thought he must be a workman. The lad

remembered that the man had a reddish face and was dressed in a long brown coat.'

I glanced at Holmes. The description of the murderer tallied exactly with his own, but there was no trace of satisfaction upon his face.

'Did you find anything in the room that could give a clue?' he asked.

'Nothing,' said Lestrade. 'Drebber's purse was in his pocket and had about eighty pounds in it. There were no papers except for a telegram with the words J. H.

is in Europe but unsigned. There was a glass of water on the table and on the windowsill a small ointment box containing a couple of pills.'

Holmes sprang from his chair with an exclamation of delight. 'The last link!' he cried. 'My case is complete!'

The two detectives and I stared at him in amazement.

'I now have in my hands,' said Holmes, 'all the threads that have caused such a tangle. I will give you proof of my knowledge. Have you got those pills?'

‘I have them,’ said Lestrade, producing a small white box. “Though I don’t attach any importance to them.’

Holmes took it and turned to me. ‘Now, Doctor, are these ordinary pills?’

They certainly were not. They were small, round, and pearly grey in colour – almost transparent in the light. ‘From their lightness and transparency, I should imagine that they are soluble in water,’ I said.

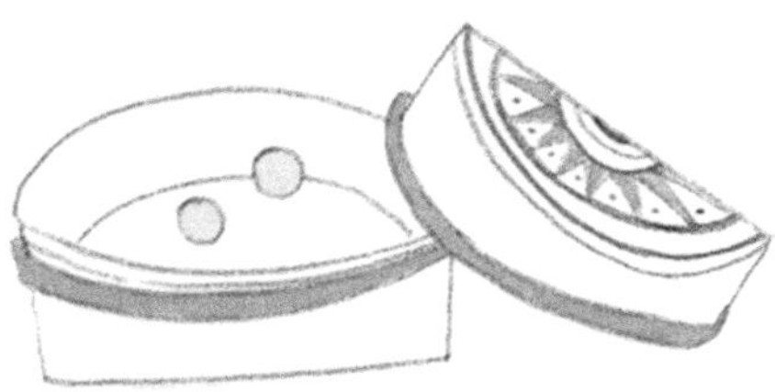

'Precisely so,' answered Holmes. Then without a word, he abruptly stood and walked over to a table where beakers and test tubes contained various coloured liquids. Filling an empty beaker with water, he dropped in one of the pills. 'You see, the doctor is right. It is dissolving already.' Then he added some liquid and sat back with a triumphant expression to watch the expected reaction.

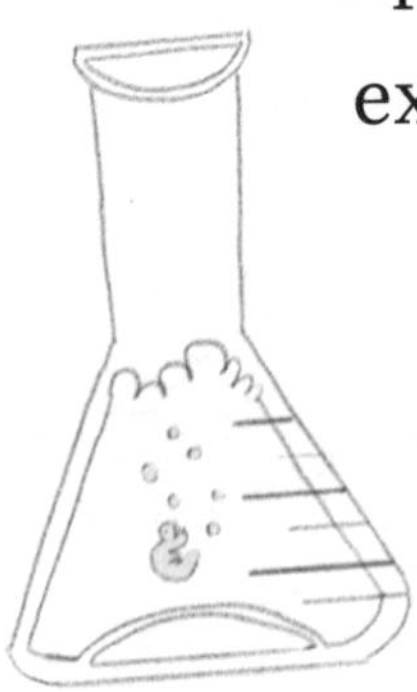

'This may be very interesting,' said Lestrade, looking

bewildered, 'but I cannot see what it has to do with the death of Mr Stangerson.'

'Patience, my friend,' Holmes responded, without taking his eyes off the beaker. 'You will soon see the reason for my experiment.'

However, nothing happened. Holmes took out his watch and stared at it as, minute by minute, there was no change in the beaker. I felt sorry for Holmes as he drummed his fingers on the table while the two detectives smiled and seemed pleased at the lack of result.

'It can't be coincidence,' he cried, at last springing from his chair and pacing wildly up and down the room. 'The very pills that I suspected in the case of Drebber are found after the death of Stangerson, yet they seem to be perfectly safe. What can it mean? Surely my whole line of reasoning cannot have been false!'

Holmes suddenly stopped in his tracks. 'Ah! I have it! I have it!'

With a shriek of delight he took another pill from the box, dropped it into another beaker and once again added the liquid.

At once the water turned a strange red-brown colour.

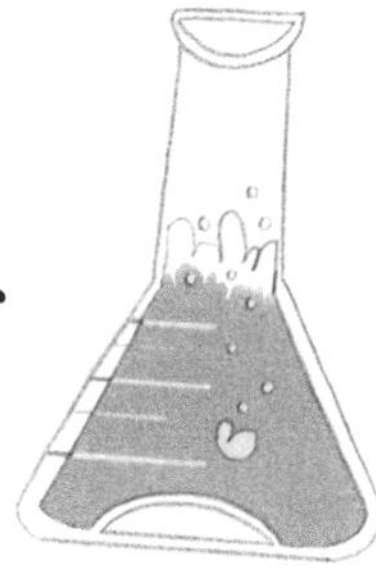

Holmes drew a long breath and wiped the sweat from his brow. 'Of course! Of the two pills in the box, one was deadly poison while the other was harmless. I ought to have known that before I even saw the box.'

The last statement was startling to me although I now realised that nothing Holmes said or did should surprise me.

'All this seems strange to you,' he said, addressing the two detectives, 'because you failed to identify the one real clue in the case. Having seized upon that, everything that has occurred since then has confirmed my suspicions. Things that puzzled you only served to enlighten me. It is a mistake to confuse strangeness with mystery. The most commonplace crime is often the most mysterious because it presents no new or special features from which deductions may be drawn. The murder would have been much more difficult had the body been found in the road without the other clues around it.

These strange details have, in fact, made the case easier.'

Mr Gregson, who had been listening with increasing impatience, could keep quiet no longer. 'Look here, Mr Sherlock Holmes, we acknowledge that you are a smart man and have your own methods of working, but we want something more than theory now. It seems that Lestrade and I were both wrong. You seem to know more than we do and so we must ask you right out. Can you name the man who did it?'

'I agree with Gregson,' said Lestrade. 'Surely you can withhold the evidence no longer.'

'Any delay in arresting the murderer,' I observed, 'may lead to his committing another crime.'

Holmes continued pacing up and down. 'There will be no more murders,' he said. 'I do know his name, but the difficulty is locating him without him suspecting that we are after him. Otherwise he may change his name and vanish. Without wanting to offend you, I consider this man to be more than a match for the force and that is why I have not asked for your help. If I fail, I shall be entirely to blame. I expect to have news very shortly.'

The detectives were far from satisfied at this. Gregson had flushed to the roots of his blond hair, while Lestrade's beady eyes glistened with curiosity and resentment.

At that moment there was a tap on the door and in came Wiggins, one of the street boys.

'Please, sir,' he said. 'I have the cab downstairs.'

'Good boy,' said Holmes,

taking a pair of steel handcuffs from a drawer. 'See how well the spring works on these?'

'Our old ones are good enough,' remarked Lestrade, 'if we can only find the man to put them on.'

'The cabman may as well help me with my boxes. Just ask him to come up, Wiggins,' said Holmes.

I was surprised at his words for I had no idea that he was about to set out on a journey and the only luggage was a small suitcase, which Holmes pulled out and began to fasten the strap as the cabman entered.

'Just give me a hand with the buckle, cabman,' he said, still struggling with it.

The cabman came forwards with a sullen, defiant expression on his face, and bent down to help. In an instant there was a sharp click, the jangling of metal, and Holmes sprang to his feet again.

'Gentlemen,' he cried with flashing eyes, 'let me introduce you to Mr Jefferson Hope, the murderer of Enoch Drebber and Joseph Stangerson.'

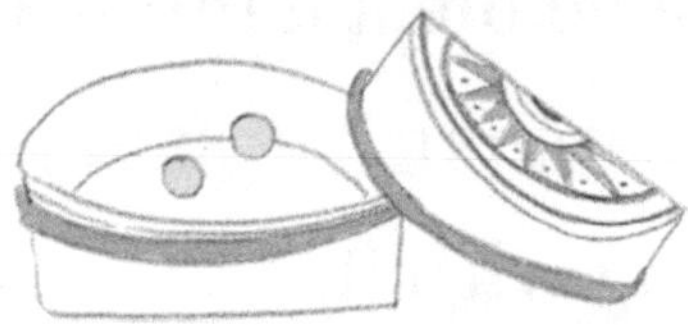

Chapter Eleven

The whole thing happened so quickly that I had no time to realise it but I will always remember Holmes' triumphant expression and the ring of his voice, and the dazed face of the cabman as he stared at the glittering handcuffs, which had appeared, as if by magic, on his wrists.

For a moment we must have been like a group of statues,

then, with a roar of fury, the prisoner wrenched himself free of Holmes' grasp and hurled himself at the window. Before he was quite through the now shattered window, Gregson, Lestrade and Holmes sprang upon him and dragged him back into the room. So powerful and so fierce was he that the four of us were shaken off again and again. His face and hands were terribly cut by the glass but loss of blood had no effect on his strength of resistance. It was not until Lestrade got hold of his collar and half choked him that he realised he had lost the struggle. Even then we did not feel safe until we had tied his hands and feet. Then we all rose to our feet, breathless and panting.

'We have his cab,' said Holmes. 'It will serve to take him to Scotland Yard.'

Finding himself powerless, our prisoner smiled in a friendly manner and said he hoped he hadn't hurt us. 'If you'll untie my legs I'll walk down,' he said.

Gregson and Lestrade exchanged glances as if they didn't trust him, but Holmes loosened the bonds around his ankles. He stood up and stretched and I thought that I had never seen a more powerfully built man. His dark, sunburned face showed determination that was as formidable as his strength.

'If there is a vacancy for a chief of police, I reckon you are the man for it,' he said, looking at Holmes with admiration. 'The way you kept on my trail was astounding.'

'I can drive,' said Lestrade.

'Good,' said Holmes. 'Gregson, you can come inside with me – and you too, Watson. You have taken an interest in the case and may as well stick with it.'

I agreed gladly and we all went downstairs together, the prisoner making no attempt at escape. We stepped into his cab and Lestrade mounted to the driver's seat and whipped up the horse.

When we reached the police station an officer noted down the man's name and the names of the men he had murdered. 'The prisoner will appear before the magistrate within a week,' he said. 'In the meantime, Mr Jefferson Hope, have you anything that you wish to say?'

'I have a good deal to say,' Hope said slowly. 'I want to tell you gentlemen all about it.'

'Hadn't you better reserve that for your trial?' asked the inspector.

'I may never be tried,' he answered. 'And I'm not thinking of suicide.' He turned to me with his fierce, dark eyes. 'Are you a doctor?'

'I am,' I answered.

'Then put your hand here,' he said with a smile, and pointed to his chest.

I did so, and noticed an extraordinary throbbing going on inside. 'Why! You have an aortic aneurysm! The main artery from your heart is bulging like a balloon.'

'That is so,' he said. 'I went to see a doctor last week and he said that it could burst at any time. I've done my work and don't care how soon I go, but I should like to cxplain why I did what I did.

I don't want to be remembered as a common cut-throat.'

The inspector and the two detectives had a hurried discussion.

'Do you consider, Doctor, that there is immediate danger of death?' asked the inspector.

'Most certainly there is,' I answered.

'In that case it is clearly our duty to take his statement now. You may give your account, sir, but it will be written down.'

Hope sat down wearily and I suspected that the struggle had worn him out. 'Since I'm on the brink of death, I am unlikely to lie to you. Every word is the absolute truth.'

He leaned back in his chair and began his tale in a calm manner, while Lestrade wrote it all down in his notebook.

'The men I killed were guilty of the murder of two people – a father and his daughter. So much time has passed that no court of law would convict them. I determined that I should be judge, jury and executioner, all rolled into one. You'd have done the same if you were in my place.

'The girl I spoke of was to have married me twenty years ago. I first met her just outside one of the great cities of America. It was a warm June morning and she was on her way to the city. There were droves of sheep and cattle coming in from pasture land. Through these galloped Lucy Ferrier, her face flushed with the exercise and her long chestnut hair floating out behind. I was immediately

struck by her beauty and skilled horsemanship, but as she tried to pass a drove of fierce-eyed, long-horned bullocks, she was suddenly surrounded by the beasts. Her horse must have been speared by a horn, for it reared

up on its hind legs, threatening to unseat her. The situation could have been fatal, so I seized her horse and forced a way through the cattle.'

Hope shifted in his chair and we waited for him to continue.

'She appeared not to be hurt. I returned to my companions and we continued on our way to prospect for silver, but I could not get the girl out of my mind. I was sure that she was John Ferrier's daughter since I had seen her leaving his house. He and my father were friends.

'That night I called on John Ferrier and he told me their story. In 1847 he and his family had joined a small group heading west looking for a place to settle, but the land was harsh and unforgiving and there were bears and bands of Indians. Ferrier and a small girl, Lucy, were the last survivors of the group. With the last of his strength he had carried her up to a high place to look out onto the plain in his search for water. He had given the last of the food to Lucy and they lay there, preparing to die, when a huge band of people from a religious group happened upon them and they were saved from certain death. Drebber and Stangerson were part of that group.

'This group took them in on condition that they follow their religion and way of life, which Ferrier was glad to do. Over the years he worked hard and built a farm, which prospered exceedingly. He adopted Lucy as his daughter and she grew up to become the young woman that I met.

'I visited Ferrier and Lucy many times until, at last, I had to leave for a couple of months. But first I asked Lucy to wait for me and we would be married on my return. She readily agreed and I tore myself away before my resolve should change.'

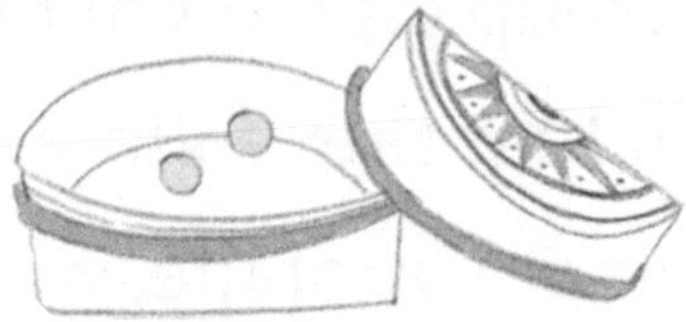

Chapter Twelve

Hope paused to take a sip of the tea that had been brought for us all. I glanced at Holmes, whose expression was one of puzzlement as if he were trying to fit the story together with the facts we knew.

'After two months I returned,' Hope continued. 'The journey was hard and for forty-eight hours I had no food so I arrived exhausted on their doorstep, but not before observing that the house was being watched by sinister men. I crawled the last few yards to avoid being seen. Ferrier gave me cold meat and bread and as soon as I'd eaten I asked after Lucy.

'"She does not know the danger," Ferrier told me, and seized my hand. He explained that Lucy had been promised to another man and the marriage would take place soon. John had been accused of breaking his promise to comply with the group's way of life, and had received a threat to their lives. These people were ruthless and cruel. They had given

Lucy twenty-eight days to choose between two young men, sons of the leaders, as was traditional in their society. Neither did he wish upon his daughter. I later found out that Drebber and Stangerson were these men. Each day the Ferriers found a number painted upon wall or floor, counting down from twenty-eight.

'I told John that I had a mule and two horses waiting in the Eagle Ravine and that we must leave immediately. He woke Lucy and we crept to a side window since the front and rear approaches were being watched. I knew that Ferrier was sad to leave the farm that he had built up from nothing but there was no choice.

'We opened the window carefully and waited until a cloud had darkened the night. One by one we climbed out into the little garden. Then we crouched low and scuttled to the shelter of a hedge. It was then that I heard the sad hooting of a mountain owl quite nearby, followed by another not far away. I realised this was a signal the men watching over the house used to communicate with each other so I dragged Lucy and Ferrier further into the hedge. Two shadowy figures emerged and I heard their whispered

plans for Lucy's abduction the following night.

'Once away from the house we made good progress and found the mule and horses waiting, and so we headed for the mountains. For two days we continued, by that time running out of provisions, so I left to hunt for some food. When I returned some five hours later they were gone and all that was left was a little pile of glowing ashes where the fire had been. Nearby was a newly dug grave. A stick had been planted on it, with a sheet of paper stuck in the fork. The paper read:

John Ferrier
Died August 4th 1860

'There was no sign of Lucy and, after some days, I met a man I knew on my way back towards the city. "You are mad to come here," he said. "There is a warrant against you for helping the Ferriers get away." When I asked about Lucy he told me that she had been married

to Drebber on the previous day. But not a month later came the devastating news that she had died of despair. On the eve of her funeral, not caring for my own safety, I strode into the chamber where she lay mourned by some other women. I stooped and kissed her cold forehead, then took up her gentle hand and removed the wedding ring from it. She should not be buried with that ring, which only proved ownership by a man who thought nothing for her.'

At this Holmes nodded and I realised the significance of the mysterious gold ring. My heart went out to this man who had loved a woman so much that he had given his own life to avenge her brief and unhappy one.

'Pray continue,' urged Holmes.

'My whole life thereafter was focussed on avenging her death and hunting down Drebber and Stangerson. After many years I happened to spot one of them in Cleveland but he saw me too and reported me to

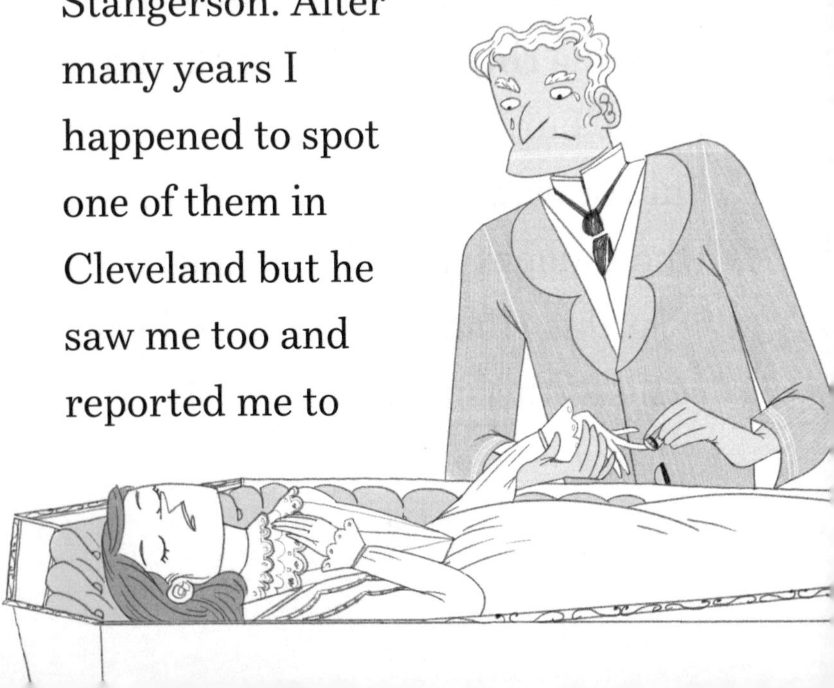

the police. When I was released, I heard that they had departed for Europe. Eventually I followed them to London, but it was not easy. They were rich and I was poor. Then I had the idea of applying to be a cab driver, since driving and riding are second nature to me. The hardest job was finding my way about, but I had a map beside me, and once I had spotted the principal hotels and stations, I got on pretty well.

'At last I found out where the two gentlemen were living – in a boarding house in Camberwell. I had grown a beard to disguise myself and I followed them relentlessly, awaiting my opportunity. It was easy to follow them in my cab without arousing suspicion, although they must have suspected there was some danger because they would never go out alone and never after nightfall.

Drebber was drunk most of the time but Stangerson was always alert and I followed them for two weeks before I saw my chance.

'I was passing their lodgings one evening when a cab stopped outside and luggage was brought out, followed by Drebber and Stangerson. I stayed close behind their cab,

which stopped at Euston Station, where they alighted. I left a boy to hold my horse and followed them. I heard them ask for the Liverpool train but the guard told them that it had just gone and there wouldn't be another one for several hours. I was so close that I could hear everything they said. Drebber said he had a little business to do and would rejoin Stangerson later. The latter was not pleased since they had agreed not to separate but they finally settled that if they should miss the last train, they would meet at Halliday's Private Hotel.

'Here was my moment at last, after all these years, but I was not too hasty and planned my actions carefully. I knew of a house in Brixton that was vacant – a gentleman I had taken there to look at the property had dropped the keys in my cab. Now I had to solve the problem of getting Drebber there, so I followed him. After stopping at several liquor shops he staggered in his walk and eventually hailed a hansom cab. I followed in my own cab and was astounded when he arrived back at his lodgings.'

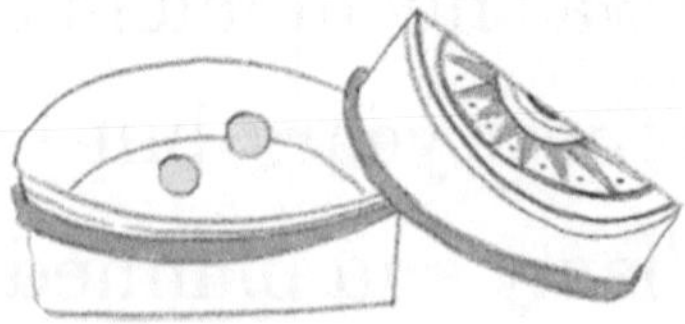

Chapter Thirteen

At this point, Hope looked up and asked for a drink of water. 'My mouth gets dry with all the talking.'

I handed him the glass and he drank it down.

'After a quarter of an hour or so, there was a commotion in the house and two men burst through the door, one of whom was Drebber and the other a stranger. This fellow had Drebber by the collar and flung

him into the street. Drebber staggered a little way down the road and then saw my cab and jumped in.

'"Drive me to Halliday's Private Hotel," he said.

'When I had him inside my cab my heart jumped with such joy that I thought my aneurysm might burst there and then. I had no intention of killing him in cold blood, you understand. He would have a chance to live. Some years ago I was working as sweeper at a laboratory when a professor was showing his students a chemical extracted from some South American arrow poison. I helped myself to a little of it and always kept the boxes with me.

'It was nearing one in the morning and was a bleak, wild night, blowing hard and raining in torrents. There was not a soul to be seen. Drebber was huddled in a drunken sleep and I shook him by the arm. "It's time to get out," I said. Thinking he was at the hotel, he got out and followed me up the garden. I opened the door and helped him inside and into the front room.

'"It's dark," he said, stamping about.

"We'll soon have light," I said, striking a match and lighting a wax candle that I had brought with me. "Now, Enoch Drebber," I said, turning to him and holding the candle to my face. "Who am I?"

'He gazed at me and slowly an expression of horror came over his face. At that sight, I smiled: vengeance would be sweet.

'"What do you think of Lucy Ferrier now?" I cried, locking the door and shaking the key in his face. "Punishment has been slow in coming, but it has overtaken you at last."

'"Would you murder me?" he asked.

'"There is no murder," I said. "Who talks of murdering a mad dog? What mercy had you upon my poor darling when you broke her innocent heart?"

'I thrust the box before him. "Let God judge between us. Choose and eat. There is death in one pill and life in the other. I shall take what you leave. Let us see if there

is justice upon the earth, or if we are ruled by chance."

'He cowered away with wild cries and prayers for mercy but at last he obeyed me. I swallowed the remaining pill and we stood facing one another in silence for a minute or two, waiting to see who was to live and who was to die. I will never forget the look on his face when the first warning pangs told him that the poison was in his system. I laughed as I saw it and held Lucy's wedding ring in front of his eyes. The poison worked quickly. He staggered and then fell heavily to the floor. He was dead!'

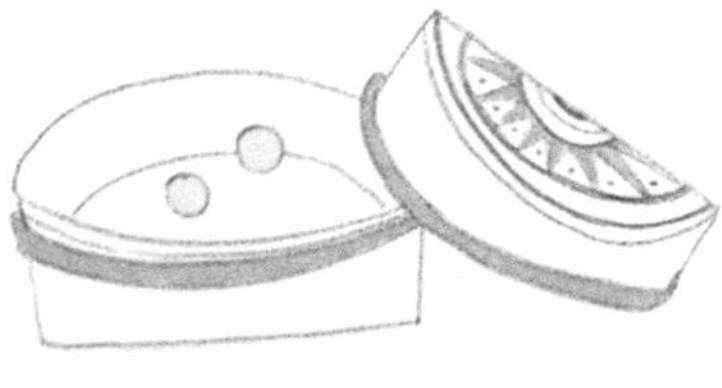

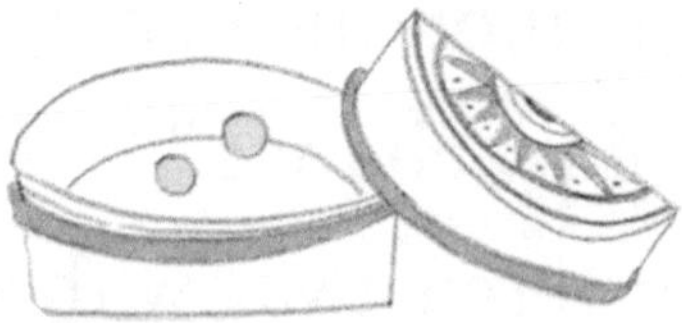

Chapter Fourteen

We were all silent as we listened to this horrible tale and saw what twenty years of bitterness and hate could do to a man.

'Blood started streaming from my nose,' he went on, 'and I don't know what made me write upon the wall with it. Perhaps it was to put the police on the wrong track. I remembered a case in New York where a German had written the word RACHE, which had confounded the police and the newspapers. Then I left but had only driven a short distance when I discovered that Lucy's ring was missing from my pocket. I went back, leaving my cab in a side street. I walked straight into the arms of the police and had to pretend to be hopelessly drunk.'

'And Stangerson?' asked Gregson.

'Stangerson,' said Hope. 'I had to do the same for him to avenge John Ferrier's debt. I waited all day outside Halliday's Private Hotel but he didn't come out.

He was cunning, that one, and always on his guard. Early the next morning I took advantage of a ladder that was lying about and entered his room through the window. I described Drebber's death to him and gave him the same choice of pills. Instead of taking the chance I offered him, he flew at my throat and I was forced to stab him in self-defence.

'And that's about all I have to say, gentlemen. I continued to drive my cab for a few days to save enough money to take me back to America. I was standing in the yard today when a ragged youngster asked if there was a cabby called Jefferson Hope, and said that he was wanted by a gentleman from 221B Baker Street. I went round expecting no harm but the next thing I knew this young man here had bracelets on my wrists. That's my story, gentlemen. You may consider me a murderer but I think I am as much an officer of justice as you are.'

We had all sat enthralled at this exciting tale. When Hope had finished we sat silently for a few minutes in a stillness only broken by the scratching of Lestrade's pencil in his notebook.

Finally, Holmes spoke. 'Who was your accomplice who came for the ring that I advertised?'

The prisoner winked. 'I saw your advertisement and thought it may be a trick so my friend volunteered to go and see. I think you'll agree that he did it well?'

'No doubt of that,' said Holmes.

We were interrupted by the inspector. 'Now, gentlemen, on Thursday the prisoner will be brought before the magistrates, and your attendance will be required.' He rang a bell and Jefferson Hope was taken away by two officers while my friend and I made our way back to Baker Street.

By Thursday, though, we had no need to attend. The very night after his capture, Jefferson Hope's aneurysm burst and he was found the next morning on the floor of his cell with a look of self-satisfaction on his face.

'Gregson and Lestrade will be wild about his death,' said Holmes as we sat by the fire the next evening. 'A court case would have raised their reputations.'

'I don't see that they had very much to do with his capture,' I said.

'It's not what you do in this world,' said Holmes, bitterly; 'it's what you can make people believe that you have done. But I would not have missed this investigation for anything. Simple as it was, there were several most instructive points about it.'

'Simple!' I cried.

'Well, I can hardly describe it as otherwise,' said Holmes, smiling. 'Without any but the most basic deductions, I was able to lay my hands on the criminal within three days.'

'That is true,' I said.

'I have already explained that what is out of the ordinary is an advantage in solving the mystery. There is also a very useful skill, and a very easy one, that people do not practice much: the art of reasoning backwards. Few people, if you told them a result, would be able tell you the steps that led to that result. Let me show you the different steps in my reasoning.'

I sat back in my chair waiting to be enlightened.

'As you know, I approached the house on foot,' began Holmes, picking up his pipe and beginning to fill it. 'I began by examining the road where I found, as you know, the marks of a cab, which must have been there during the night. I knew it was a cab by the mark of the wheels. I then went up the path and examined the footprints. I could see the heavy tracks of the police, but underneath were the tracks of the two men who had first passed through the garden. This was my second link, which told me that there had been two visitors: one tall as shown by the length of his stride, and one fashionably dressed, going by his small and elegant boots.

'On entering the house, I perceived that the well-dressed man lay before me, leaving the tall one as the murderer. There was no wound on his body but the expression on his face showed me that he had seen his fate before it came upon him. Having sniffed the dead man's lips, I detected a sour smell and came to the conclusion that he had been poisoned.

'Now came the great question of motive. It was not robbery. Was it politics then, or a woman? Political assassins usually do their work and flee, but this man had lingered and written upon the wall. When the ring was found, it settled the question.

'I then made a careful examination of the room, which confirmed the murderer's height, the length of his nails, and the fact that he smoked Trichinopoly cigars. Since there were no signs

of a struggle, the blood must have come from the murderer. I suspected a nosebleed, so I suspected a red-faced man.

'I had already deduced that the man who had walked into the house had also driven the cab, because the marks in the road showed that the horse had wandered a little, which would not have happened had there been someone in charge of it. And what better way of tracking someone than in a cab? I assumed he would continue being a cabby for the time being to avoid suspicion, so

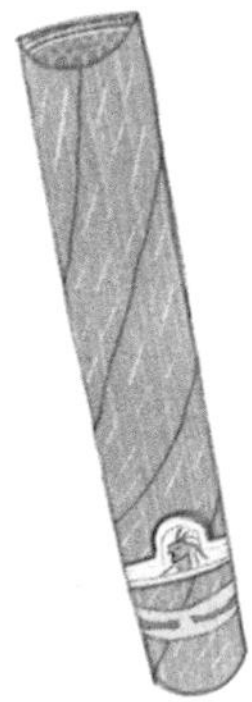

I enlisted the help of my street boys and sent them to every cab company in London until they ferreted out the man I wanted.

'The murder of Stangerson was unexpected, but through that tragedy I came into possession of the pills, which confirmed how Drebber was poisoned. You see, the whole thing is a chain of logical sequences without a break or flaw.'

'It's wonderful!' I cried. 'Your skills must be publicly recognised. You should publish an account of the case. If you won't, I will do it for you.'

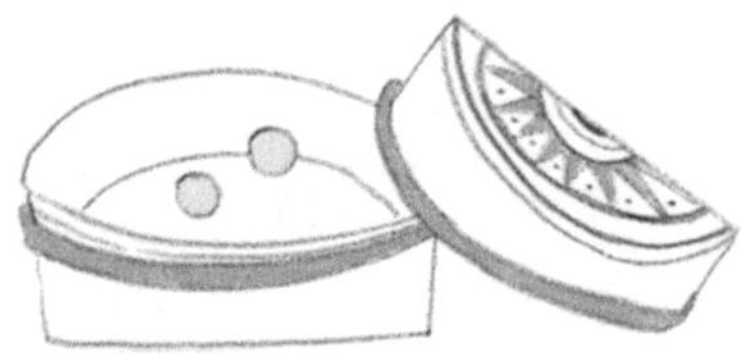

'You may do what you like, Doctor,' he answered. 'See here.' He handed me a copy of the Echo and pointed to an article.

'Didn't I tell you so when we started?' said Holmes with a laugh. 'That's the result of our study in scarlet: to get them a medal!'

'Never mind,' I answered. 'I have all the facts in my journal and the public shall know them. In the meantime you must be content at knowing your own success.'

Holmes smiled in his slightly amused, slightly smug way, leaned back in his chair, and lit his pipe.

Sherlock Holmes

World-renowned private detective Sherlock Holmes has solved hundreds of mysteries, and is the author of such fascinating monographs as *Early English Charters* and *The Influence of a Trade Upon the Form of a Hand.* He keeps bees in his free time.

Dr John Watson

Wounded in action at Maiwand, Dr John Watson left the army and moved into 221B Baker Street. There he was surprised to learn that his new friend, Sherlock Holmes, faced daily peril solving crimes, and began documenting his investigations. Dr Watson also runs a doctor's practice.